Old

Rosie

the horse

nobody

understood

Old Rosie
the horse
nobody understood

by LILIAN MOORE

and LEONE ADELSON

illustrated by Leonard Shortall

Random House, New York

for

DON

LEVENSON

WHAT a day it was going to be!
Farmer Dilly did not know it.
His horse, Rosie, did not know it.
And it was a good thing, too!
"Now see here, Rosie," said Far-
mer Dilly. "We must get to the milk

train on time today. Do you understand?"

Rosie's head went up and down.

"Nothing silly, like yesterday?" said
the farmer.

Rosie shook her head.

"And nothing like the day before
that?"

Rosie's big brown eyes seemed to
say, "Who——me?"

Just then came the long toot-toot
of a train whistle.

"There's the milk train, Rosie, still
far away. Let's go." Farmer Dilly
jumped up on the wagon. "Giddap,
old girl," he said. "First stop is at

Farmer Brown's house."

Rosie went down the road so fast that Farmer Dilly began to feel quite happy.

"Well," he said to his horse, "this is more like my good old Rosie!"

Soon they pulled up at Farmer Brown's big white house. Farmer Dilly hopped down from his seat on the wagon, and gave Rosie a pat on the head.

"I'll be right out with the milk cans, and then off we go," he told her. Farmer Dilly worked fast. He ran into the barn. He rolled out the two big milk cans that were waiting

for him. Quickly he put them into the back of the wagon. "We're right on time, Rosie. Giddap, old girl," he said.

But Rosie did not move. Farmer Dilly jumped down again and ran to look at his horse. There she stood, one foot in front of the other. Her head was resting on Farmer Brown's mail box. Her eyes were closed tight. She was fast asleep!

"Rosie, Rosie!" shouted Farmer Dilly. "Wake up! Wake up! Can't you hear the whistle? We must get

this milk to the train!"

At the word "train" Rosie's head
came up. Her eyes opened wide.
Train? Oh, yes, the train—she had to
get to the train. She must not miss it.

With a shake of her head she began
to run down the road as fast as her
old legs could go.

"Stop, stop!" cried Farmer Dilly.
"Wait for me, Rosie!" But old Rosie
did not stop. She had to get Farmer
Dilly to the milk train on time!

He ran down the road after his
wagon and jumped up on the seat.
Farmer Dilly's face was red, he was
puffing like an engine, and he was
very, very angry.

Rosie did not slow down until they
came to the next stop—Farmer Winterberry's house. They had to pick up
some milk here, too.

Farmer Dilly was going to scold
Rosie. Just then she looked around at
him as if to say, "My! Didn't I get
us here fast!" He just could not scold
her then.

Rosie had pulled up right beside
Farmer Winterberry's mail box.

"Oh, no, not this time," said

14

Farmer Dilly, still a little angry. "No mail box for you to go to sleep on. I'll fix that."

And he pulled his horse way over to the other side of the road.

Toot-toot! went the train whistle.

"There's the train, Rosie. We can still make it! I'll be right out. You be ready for me."

This time six cans were waiting for him in the back yard. To save time Farmer Dilly put them all on a hand truck. Then quickly he pushed the hand truck out to the wagon.

But where was the wagon?

And where was Rosie?

He ran down the road and looked. No wagon. He ran back up the road and looked. No Rosie. He had to find her!

Farmer Winterberry would help him. He ran up the side road to Farmer Winterberry's farm.

Then he saw Rosie.

No, she did not need a mail box.

Not at all! There she stood, close to Farmer Winterberry's old horse, Prince. With her head on Prince's back, she was fast asleep. So was Prince.

Farmer Dilly was too angry to talk. His face was as red as a tomato. He was hot and he still had work to do. Could they make the train on time? He worked as fast as he could to get Rosie back on the road and the milk

cans on the wagon.

There was no time to scold Rosie—not yet. He waited until he was on the wagon and they had started down the road again.

"Now, you silly old horse," said Farmer Dilly. "I want to tell you a thing or two. How in the——"

Toot-toot! The train whistle! Rosie's ears went back. The train must be pulling in! She could not wait to

hear what Farmer Dilly had to say. This was no time to talk. Off she went down the road, the wagon rocking from side to side.

There was the train, waiting for them. The train men called to them to hurry.

"Late again. What's the matter, Mr. Dilly?" and one of the men laughed as he began to take the milk cans off the wagon. "Did you sleep too long this morning?"

Farmer Dilly did not feel at all like laughing. "It's my old horse, Rosie." He shook his head. "I don't know what's the matter with her."

"Poor Rosie," said the man. "Maybe
she is too old to pull that wagon any
more. Is that it, old girl?" The train
men liked Rosie. They always petted

her and gave her good things to eat.

When all the milk cans had been put on the train, the train began to pull away.

"Better be on time tomorrow, Mr. Dilly," called one of the men. "We can't wait for you again, you know."

All the way home Farmer Dilly thought and thought. He looked at Rosie. Maybe she *was* too old now to pull a milk wagon. What would he do without Rosie? But what would he do with Rosie if the milk train did not wait?

All the way home he thought and thought. When he got home he put

Rosie in the barn. Then he went to talk to Mrs. Dilly.

"I think Rosie is too old to work any more," he said to his wife. "From now on she's going to rest. No more work for her. She can sleep all she wants to and eat all she likes. She can stay in the barn or roll in the grass."

"Then who will pull the milk wagon?" asked Mrs. Dilly.

"No one—I'm going to buy a truck this very day," he told her.

"Poor old Rosie," said Grandma Dilly. "Horses are like people. When they get old they can't help us any more. Then we have to help them."

"Yes," said Farmer Dilly. "Rosie has worked long and well. Now she's going to have a good time."

And Rosie *did* have a good time— for a few days. How nice it was to sleep late every morning! What fun it was to run and chase the rabbits! How good it was to roll in the cool

grass and feel it on her hot back! She had nothing to do all day but to sleep, to run, to eat, and to play.

But every day she did the same things.

And after a while it was not quite so much fun to have nothing more to do. Nothing to do but run after rabbits. Nothing to do but sleep in the barn or roll in the grass—all by herself.

One morning she stood and watched Farmer Dilly drive off in his new red

truck. He had no time for Rosie now.
No time to say, "Good morning, Rosie.
How's my old girl today?" No time
to pet her and give her something
sweet to eat. Now it was the truck
that went down the good hard road in
the quiet morning. It was the truck
that saw all the things and people on
the way. But who would want to say
"Good morning" to a truck? And how
could a truck say anything to Prince

as it went by the Winterberry farm?
How could the friendly train men pet
the new red truck?

Rosie missed all these things. She
missed the run down the road to the
milk train, and all the things and
people on the way. But most of all
she missed Farmer Dilly.

Rosie did not know it, but she was
lonesome.

Perhaps that is why she came to do
the things she did.

It all began because one day Rosie
thought she just *had* to see Farmer
Dilly. She could not get out through
the gate—the gate was closed. She

could not jump over the fence—the
fence was too high. But away off in the
field was an old stone wall that was
falling down. Rosie looked at it for a

long time. Yes, it would be easy to
jump over that. She gave a little run
and a jump. Over she went, and down
the road to the farm house.

How happy she was! She was going to see the Dilly family. And how happy they would be to see her. They must miss her, too.

Oh dear, there was no one in the front yard. Maybe there was someone in the back yard. She looked—no one was there. Then Rosie saw that the cellar door was open. Perhaps she would find someone down there. She walked over and looked down the stairs. It was very quiet, but sniff— sniff! What was that wonderful smell? It was the most wonderful smell of all —the strong sweet smell of fresh apples.

Do you know how good a hot dog smells to a hungry boy? That is how those apples smelled to Rosie. Before she knew it she was down the steps and in the cellar. And there they were —a pan full of big red apples!

How good they were! Every one of them—down to the very last one. Rosie stood there, full of apples, feeling good and a little sleepy. She heard people walking around upstairs and talking. That was good, too. Her head dropped down, her eyes closed, and soon she was fast asleep.

Up in the kitchen Grandma Dilly was about to bake a pie.

"Ah!" said Mr. Dilly. "Pie for supper—I hope it's apple pie."

"That's just what it is going to be!"
Grandma laughed. "I have a nice pan
of my best apples down in the cellar.
I have been keeping them just for a
pie," she said. "I'll go down and get
them now."

Grandma was halfway down the
cellar steps when Mr. and Mrs. Dilly
heard her scream.

All Grandma saw in the cellar at
first was a big dark Something. All
Rosie knew was that a scream woke
her out of a quiet nap. Before Grandma knew that the Something was only

Rosie, she had run all the way back up to the kitchen. And before Rosie knew that it was only Grandma, she had been frightened out of the cellar and was running down the road back to the barn.

Farmer Dilly looked out the window just in time to see Rosie go down the road.

"There goes Rosie!" cried Farmer Dilly. "What has she been up to?"

As soon as they found the apples gone they understood what had happened.

"My, what a fright she gave me!" said Grandma Dilly again and again. "And eating all my best apples, too!"

"That's a funny thing for Rosie to do," said Farmer Dilly. "She never did anything like that before."

Mrs. Dilly was puzzled, too. "She gets plenty to eat. Why is she so

greedy?" she said. "I guess we will just have to keep the cellar door closed."

Rosie had been so frightened that for a few days she stayed close to the barn. But soon she began to feel lonesome again.

No one came near her. She did not want to run or play or roll in the grass. She did not even want to chase the funny little rabbits that ran by. More than anything, she wanted to be with someone she loved. So one

day Rosie jumped over the wall again
and trotted down the road to the farm
house.

There was a car in front of the
house, but no people. Rosie trotted
around to the back of the house. Nobody there! Nothing to do but wait.
She looked around. There were some
pretty red flowers in the window box.
M-m-m—they smelled good. M-m-m
—they tasted good, too. She ate them
all, and then put her head through

the open window. Maybe there were some more inside. Rosie looked around, and then she saw the Thing!

It was a pretty yellow Thing, and on it was a big red flower. How nice! More flowers! They were not good to eat, but the yellow Thing smelled just like hay. It tasted just like hay, too, so Rosie ate it all up. No—not quite all, for almost at the last bite, Mrs. Dilly walked into the room with her friend, Mrs. Winterberry.

How glad Rosie was to see someone at last! She put her head as far into

the room as she could, hoping Mrs. Dilly would pet her and say, "Hello, Rosie." But all at once there was a loud cry from Mrs. Winterberry.

"Oh, look—my hat—she's eating my new hat! Get my hat!"

Poor Rosie! They rushed at her so fast that she was frightened. She pulled her head out of the window, turned, and ran down the road, jumped over the wall, and went right into the barn.

When Farmer Dilly got home that night, what a story he heard! Mrs. Dilly was quite upset.

"It was Mrs. Winterberry's very best hat," she told him. "The one with the big red flower!"

Farmer Dilly tried not to laugh, but he could not help it. He laughed and laughed.

"It's not funny," said Mrs. Dilly. "Mrs. Winterberry is very angry."

"Well," said Farmer Dilly, still laughing, "I always thought that was a mighty funny hat."

"Maybe so," said Grandma, "but I'd still like to know—what *is* the matter with that horse? Coming right to the house! Eating my best apples! Eating Mrs. Winterberry's best hat!"

"I told you she was a greedy old horse," said Mrs. Dilly, still upset about the hat.

"Yes, sir, that was some hat!" said Farmer Dilly, and he laughed again.

But a few days later, Farmer Dilly did not laugh. He was as angry as could be, for Rosie came to see the family once again.

This time she did not come to the cellar door. She had been frightened there. Nor did she come to the back door. Something had happened to her there, too. This time she came right up the front steps and into the house, to visit the Dillys.

How cool it was in the big front room! And how cool the floor looked. Rosie's back was hot from the sun,

and the floor seemed just the place to rub her wet back. So she did. She rolled back and forth on the floor. Ah-h-h! That was good!

Suddenly everything happened at once.

BANG! Rosie's foot hit the table!

CRASH! Down came the table with everything on it! BANG! THUMP! BUMP! CRASH! SMASH! Oh-h-h-h-h!

What a sight for the Dillys when they came running into the room! The table was on its side, the lamp was broken, and the box of candy was rolling all over the floor.

There sat Rosie, in the middle of it all, trying to see Farmer Dilly from under the lamp shade which sat on one ear.

"You crazy horse!" shouted the farmer. "Look what you've done! Get
out! Get out before——"

Rosie did not wait to hear any

more. Farmer Dilly's face was so angry that for the first time she was afraid of him. She ran back to the barn as fast as she could go.

"Just look at this room!" cried Farmer Dilly. "This beats anything she has ever done!"

"Well," said Mrs. Dilly, "maybe you won't laugh at her this time. Look at our table, and the lamp. And the candy—that must be what she came for!"

"What are we going to do with that horse?" asked Grandma.

"Do?" said the farmer. "I'll tell you what I'm going to do. I'm going to

sell Rosie tomorrow morning. That's what I'm going to do. First thing tomorrow I'll sell Rosie."

Rosie did not know what was going to happen the next day but she was very unhappy. Why couldn't she and Farmer Dilly have good times together any more? Why did something always go wrong? All she wanted was to be near the family. But every time she went to see them someone got angry at her. Someone always shouted at her. Nobody petted her any more. It almost seemed that no one loved her any more.

Rosie walked out of the barn and

looked over the fence at the house. It
was a beautiful night. The stars were
out and the moon was bright. The old
horse could not sleep. All she could
think of was Farmer Dilly's angry

face. She had a feeling that she must go back to the house. They must not be so angry at her.

Once more she jumped over the wall and walked slowly and sadly to the house. The house was dark and very quiet. Everyone was asleep. Everything was closed tight to keep her out. How lonely she was!

But there! One window was open in the back of the house. And something was moving in the window. Maybe someone was up, after all. Could it be Grandma? No—too big. Could it be Mrs. Dilly? No, it was a man. Oh, it must be Farmer Dilly! But no, this

was a fat man. Rosie did not know
who it was but she was so glad to see
someone at last. Maybe the man had
an apple for her. Maybe he would
even pet her!

Rosie walked up to the window. It
was not a very big window and the
man was getting out a little at a time.
First came a leg. Then his shoulder.
Rosie came closer to look. When the
man turned to jump, he found himself looking right into Rosie's big
brown eyes. He was so surprised that
he let go, and fell right back into the
room! Now where is he? thought
Rosie. She put her head through the

open window. There he was, sitting
on the kitchen floor.

Rosie made a friendly noise.

"Sh! Nice horsey!" the man whis-

pered. "Go back to your barn like a good horse."

Rosie nodded her head to show the man that she was glad he liked her and to tell him she liked him, too.

"No, no! Go away!" the man whispered again. "Go away like a good girl."

Rosie tried to get closer to this nice man.

"Get away from that window, you stupid horse!" the man said, getting angry. "I've got to get out of here!"

But Rosie just stood at the window, trying to make friends.

Suddenly the man saw the other

kitchen window. He ran to open it.

This is a good game! thought Rosie.
So she trotted around the house to the
other window, too. The man was almost out of this window when Rosie
got there. She pulled at his leg play-
fully as if to say, "Here I am!"

"Ouch! Let go of my leg!" the man
cried out. "Let go or I'll fall!"

And he did! Right out of the win-

dow and right on top of Grandma
Dilly's flower pots. CRASH! BANG!
went the man. SMASH! BANG! went
the flower pots!

Suddenly three windows opened
upstairs.

"Who's there?" called Farmer Dilly.

"What's going on down there?"
called Grandma Dilly.

Rosie looked up. There was her family! She was so glad to see them that she forgot all about the man.

"Who's that down there?" called Farmer Dilly.

"There's a man running away!" screamed Mrs. Dilly.

"Catch him! Catch him!" cried Grandma.

But by the time they all got downstairs and turned on the lights, the man had run down the road and was out of sight.

"Look!" said Grandma Dilly. "The kitchen windows are open!"

"Our house has been robbed!" cried

Mrs. Dilly. "Oh! Oh! My clock! My good spoons! Where are they?"

"Maybe they are in here," said Farmer Dilly, picking up a brown bag from the floor. "It looks as if the robber had to go in a hurry. He didn't have time to take this with him." He opened the bag, and there were the spoons and the clock. And then he held up an old tin box. "Am I glad to see this!" he said.

"Why should anyone want to take that old thing?" asked Mrs. Dilly.

Farmer Dilly opened the box. "Because it has all this money in it! I was going to take it to the bank in

the morning. It's a good thing that robber was frightened away!"

"What ever do you suppose frightened him?" Grandma wanted to know.

"It must have been Rosie!" said Mrs. Dilly. "When we looked out, she was standing by the window."

"Good old Rosie!" said Farmer Dilly. "Where is she now?"

Rosie was back in the barn. She had seen the family come out to the yard. But they had not talked to her. No one seemed to care about her. So she had gone sadly away.

And then suddenly the barn door opened. There they stood—Farmer Dilly, Mrs. Dilly, and Grandma Dilly, smiling at her. In Farmer Dilly's hand there were two big red apples.

"Here, old Rosie," he said in his old friendly way. "If not for you, our house would have been robbed of many things tonight. Thank you, old girl."

Rosie put out her head and sniffed at the apples, but she did not eat them. She took a few steps until she stood close to Farmer Dilly. Then she put her old head down on his shoulder. Rosie was happy again.

"Why, look!" said Mrs. Dilly. "Rosie's not eating the apples. That's funny!"

Grandma Dilly shook her head. "No," she said. "It's not funny at all.

I think I know why Rosie has been doing such silly things. She didn't come for apples, or for Mrs. Winterberry's hat, or for candy. She isn't greedy. She's just lonely, that's all. That's why she came to the house again and again."

"And each time we frightened her away," said Mrs. Dilly sadly.

"That was no way to treat an old friend, was it, Rosie?" said Farmer Dilly. "It wasn't very kind to leave you all alone, was it?" He patted her head. "I know what we can do," he said. "We'll put you in that field right next to the house. Then we can

talk to you whenever we pass by, and you can watch us coming and going."

"Why, yes!" cried Mrs. Dilly. "And at night we can take you back to the barn to sleep where it's warm. How's that, Rosie dear?"

But Rosie did not hear Mrs. Dilly. She was eating the big red apples now. She had her family around her, and they loved her again.

That was enough for old Rosie!

Bambi's Children

By FELIX SALTEN

Adapted by ALLEN CHAFFEE

★

Illustrated by PHOEBE ERICKSON

Prepared under the supervision of JOSETTE FRANK,
Children's Book Adviser of the Child Study Association of America

★

RANDOM HOUSE · NEW YORK

This book is a brief retelling of *Bambi's Children*, especially designed for children aged four to seven. When the children are a little older, they will want to read the whole story, many times longer than this, just as it was written by Felix Salten. Originally published by The Bobbs-Merrill Company, Inc., Indianapolis and New York, it is now available in a reprint published by Grosset & Dunlap, Inc., of New York.

BAMBI'S young son Geno stood beside his mother. Pale stars gleamed, but he could smell the coming dawn. Soon the forest would drowse warm with sunshine.

Mother Faline's smooth coat was red-brown like the forest floor. But Geno and his twin sister Gurri had spots like bits of sunlight. Not even the Fox could have seen them beneath the bushes.

"Time for bed now," Faline told them gently.

"I won't go to bed!" Geno stamped small hoofs on the winding path.

"What's that?" a bird called.

The Jay, peering, bright-eyed, screeched, "It's Faline, the deer! Faline and her children."

Crows came flapping from their nest. "Spoiled brats!" they called.

"You ugly black things!" Geno stamped again.

3

Faline turned big brown eyes to the treetops. "You see, Geno, what they think? Remember, you are the son of Bambi!"

"Ho, ho, ho!" the crows laughed. "Teach him manners, then."

The Woodpecker, drumming on the old oak tree, called, "That's right, Faline. Or he'll have no friends when he needs them."

Geno gave a side jump. It nearly knocked his sister off her slender legs. "Someone's coming," he squealed. His black muzzle shook, and his ears turned toward the sound.

"Hush!" Faline told him. "It's only a little skunk."

"He smells!" Gurri held her breath.

"That's how he protects himself," Faline told her. "He doesn't have to run, and hide, and watch, as we do."

Faline settled down on folded legs. "Come, children."

They snuggled close to her warm body. She knew the Jay and the Woodpecker would warn them if harm came near.

"Tell us a story," the fawns begged, sleepily.

"Well," Faline began, "my brother Gobo was small for his age, and when winter came——"

"What's winter?" Geno asked.

"Winter," Faline told them, "is the time when there isn't much to eat. Trees are bare, and the sky is gray, like the back of a fish. Then one day the snow comes." Faline shivered.

"What is snow?" Gurri whispered.

"Snow," Faline told them, "comes falling from the sky. It falls and falls, till it lies deep. Then we have to scrape it away with our fore hoofs to find the grass."

She went on with her story. "That winter the snow got so deep we had to jump from place to place. But Gobo wasn't strong enough to bound above the snow drifts.

"One day HE came."

"The man with the thunder-stick?" Geno asked; and the hair pricked on the back of his neck.

"Yes," Faline whispered. "When HE came we had to run. Only Gobo couldn't. But your father could leap high drifts." Faline's eyes shone with pride.

"Gobo was left behind, and we didn't know what had happened to him. Then one day Gobo came back. He told how the man had dragged him from the snow bank and fed him."

5

At that moment a shot rang through the still forest. The fawns sprang to their feet, trembling.

"The thunder-stick!" Gurri began to cry. "Maybe it was Father that got shot!"

"No, dear," Faline told her. "Bambi's too clever to let the hunters find him."

Just then Perri, the squirrel, came leaping through the branches overhead. "No need to worry," she chattered. "HE'S just teaching the Boy to shoot at a mark."

The warm gold of sunshine spread along the forest floor, while the deer slept. Trees spread their leaves to its warmth. Bees hummed and birds sang. The Hare stood up, wiggling his bunny nose, then hopped along to find a dandelion. The sun, swinging across the sky, measured off the day.

WHEN, at last, they woke, it was evening. Faline led the fawns to the meadow. But there she waited, shoulder-high in fern, to test the air with her nose.

"There's nothing there," a bird called.

"Nothing to harm us," Perri said, leaping to the branch of an elm tree. She sat, her tail spread above her, paws folded on her chest, eating a nut.

Step by step Faline tiptoed into the tall grass. "You can come now," she called softly.

Geno and Gurri bounded to her side.

7

From across the meadow, another forest mother came, leading her fawns. It was Lana and Boso and their mother Rolla. Gurri sprang to greet them, and Geno followed with timid leaps.

Something sat half hidden in a clump of grass. "What is it?" the fawns asked each other.

Geno sniffed at the odd creature. "It pricks!" he cried.

It was a young porcupine. He raised his quills. "*Will* you leave me alone?" he asked crossly.

"Danger! Danger!" Gurri called.

The fawns raced across the meadow. Geno was fastest. "What is it?" he gasped.

"I was only joking." Gurri smiled. "I wanted to show them *my* brother could run the fastest."

The two mothers had their heads together, talking.

"Bambi doesn't come to see you very often, does he?" Rolla asked.

"He is the leader," Faline said quietly. "He must keep watch over us all."

"Doesn't he ever come to see the children?" Rolla wanted to know.

"He comes in the daytime when they are asleep," Faline told her.

"You mean, they have never *seen* their father?" Rolla asked.

"No," Faline admitted. "But they're young yet. I know he's watching out for our safety. But he has the whole herd to guard."

"Don't you ever call him?" Rolla asked.

"We're not supposed to," Faline explained.

It was dark now. An Owl called, "Hhaah-ah, hahaha, haah-ah!" The moon threw a silver light on the drinking pool. Bats zig-zagged after gnats. Fireflies glowed, and the fawns raced and butted each other about. Their small heads were hornless.

The two mothers fed till dawn came again. Then Faline led her children home. A Hare called greetings as they passed. His whiskers trembled. "Look out for the Fox!" he warned.

"Huh!" said Geno. "I can run faster than any fox."

The Hare wiggled his ears. "Do you hear anything, Ma'am?"

Faline listened. "No," she told him gently. "Don't worry."

That day she and her children slept, lulled by the sounds of the Woodpecker hammering at the bark of a tree.

Suddenly she found herself wide awake. Geno and Gurri
sprang to their feet. Someone was near.

"It's your Father," Faline told them happily.

The fawns could see nothing, but Faline walked to where
the bushes were thickest. "Greetings, Bambi!"

The answer came in a deep voice. "Greetings, my love!"

The great buck raised his head. His mighty antlers were
branched, and armed with long bright points. He stepped into
the clearing. He looked the Prince that he was.

"Children!" His dark eyes looked them over proudly.

"Father!" Geno and Gurri spoke together.

"My son," said Bambi, "you must be more polite to everyone. You may need friends some day."

Geno hung his head.

"And Gurri, be more careful. Sometimes you are rash," Bambi told his daughter.

Then, without a sound, he disappeared.

Faline thought, "Geno is very like his father."

And the fawns told themselves with pride, "We are Bambi's children."

THE FOX lapped water at the brook. His coat was dusty.

Ducks hid among the iris.

The Hare wiggled his nose. "Oh, my soul and whiskers!" he breathed.

Faline did not move. "HE can't scent us," she whispered. "There's no breeze."

The Heron, standing on one leg, pointed his sharp bill at the Fox. "It's you," he snapped.

"Do you mind if I wet my throat?" The Fox grinned.

Gurri moved closer to watch.

When at last they lay down to sleep, Geno thought he could hear the leaves whispering, "Please give us rain."

The morning did not get brighter, as it should. Now the trees began to tremble, the tall elms first. Oaks and maples shivered, their dry leaves falling. Then came the rain.

It beat with a loud drumming. Lightning tore the sky. It flashed on Bambi, whose great antlers were gleaming. He trumpeted, "Don't be afraid, Faline. Avoid the higher trees —the poplar most of all. Keep among the bushes."

Faline sprang from her forest bed. "Come, children," she called, "hurry!"

They raced after her. They were beyond the woods when another flash came. Lightning had struck the poplar. The smell of burning wood hung on the air.

Pressed together among the bushes, Faline and the fawns felt the rain beating down upon them. But the smell of wet ferns came pleasantly. Then it was over: the sun burst out.

Gurri started toward the meadow.

"Wait!" Faline told her. Not till night came again would she let the children show themselves.

13

Happy weeks passed. The fawns' coats lost their baby spots.

Faline left more and more to her son. It was now Geno who sniffed and watched for danger. It was he who led them into the meadow when evening came. Knowing he had his mother to protect, he would glide to cover if he saw a shadow he didn't understand.

One night he heard a loud call. "Oo-y, oo-y!" It was the Screech-Owl. He sat in an apple tree. "Hi!—Scared you, didn't I?" he called.

"No," Geno lied. "I should think you'd be too old to play tricks like that."

"Too *old!*" The Owl blew his feathers out till he looked twice as big. "*You* may be old when you reach the age of two. As for *me*, I am not old. Everything is relative."

"What do you mean, 'everything is relative'?" Geno demanded. "Do you mean you're an aunt of mine, or something?"

14

"How could I be your aunt?" the Owl asked angrily. "I
never laid an egg in my life, and I don't expect to." He blinked
his eyes, and drew his hooked beak into the feathers of his
chest.

Geno saw a darker shadow at the meadow's edge. He gave
the danger signal.

"It's all right," a deep voice spoke. "It's your father."

After the greetings were over, Bambi said, "My son, the
reports I hear of you are very good now. You are learning the
way of life. And that is well, for soon your mother is going
on a journey with me."

"And leave us alone?" Geno asked.

Faline's voice was troubled. "Bambi, are you sure they are
ready?"

15

He answered, "You have taught them all you know. Now they must meet the dangers of the forest for themselves."

Gurri shivered. She would be afraid.

"Gurri," her father's voice was grave. "When you are alone, you must be twice as careful. Move up-wind always. Heed the warnings of your friends, the birds and squirrels."

Bambi turned to Geno. "Son," he said, "at the first sign of danger, make for the bushes where they're thickest. Beware, always, of HIM. Man is the only one who can kill from a distance. HE and his dogs mean danger. But they nearly always hunt by day. Night time is safest.

"One thing more. Do not call your mother. Later, she will come back to you."

Geno promised. And the next night, when he and Gurri woke, Faline was gone.

"Mother!" Gurri cried.

"Quiet!" Geno commanded.

NOW the fawns played at being grown up. They sniffed the breeze, and peered at every shadow. They came home with the first light of morning, to sleep the day away in hiding.

Perri, the squirrel, told them one evening, "Something is wrong."

"What is wrong?" Geno demanded.

"I don't know. I just feel it." Perri folded her paws on her furry chest.

"OO-y, oo-y!" the Owl screeched.

"What is it?" Gurri dashed out from her hiding place. She looked about her, curious.

Perri, in the treetop, shouted, "Back! *Back!*" but it was too late.

A Fox sprang at Gurri.

His weight bore her down. Hungry teeth bit into her shoulder. The Fox tried for her throat.

A cry of pain tore its way from her chest.

The thunder-stick roared in her ears. The Fox turned a
somersault, then lay still.

The Gamekeeper bent to look at Gurri's wound, and his blue eyes were filled with pity.

"Lucky I came along," he told himself.

He lifted the wounded fawn, and carried her away.

Geno was wild with grief. "Mother!" he called. "Mother!"

"Here I am," she said at last. "Where is your sister?"

Bambi sprang into sight. "What is it, Son?"

"Gurri—the Fox—and HE!" Geno stood in dumb misery.

Bambi, with his muzzle to the ground, moved along the path and into the dark meadow.

20

Next day the Screech-Owl floated by and settled on a branch. "It will teach her a lesson." He snapped his beak.

Faline gasped. "Is Gurri alive, do you think?"

"I don't think," the Owl snapped. "I know."

"You *know* she's alive?" Geno called.

"I do, young fellow. I have good eyesight in the *dark*, and I followed them. HE has a big sort of nest on the ground, if you could call it that; and he took Gurri in. It so happens there's an Owl I know there, already. He finds it quite comfortable. So then I flew to tell Bambi."

The Owl focused one large eye on Geno. "I always say, 'While there's life, there's hope'."

"Bless my soul and whiskers," the Hare told them. "A Field Mouse who goes there for cheese declares Gurri's there. But she can't get out."

GURRI tried to get away, but the man held her firmly. At last he set her down, and washed her wound. "Just a torn muscle. It will heal," he said. But Gurri couldn't understand.

Trembling, she got to her feet, and tried to shove her way through the vines that hemmed the place about. But they pricked her chest, and she couldn't get out.

22

Now a dog came bounding to the man. The dog sniffed at Gurri. She stood still, but her legs shook with fright.

"Come, Hector," said the man, and the dog followed as he went away.

A shower of rain fell by and by. Gurri shivered. She thought she was alone till a wild cry sounded behind her.

"Whoo-hoo-oo-oo!"

A great Horned Owl stood on a post watching her. He had a chain around one ankle. "I won't hurt you," he said. "I'm a prisoner, too." He gnashed his beak.

Gurri lay down, too unhappy to speak. Was she never to see home again? Worn out, she slept at last.

Hours later, she opened her eyes. Sunlight made the valley a golden bowl. On one side rose the dark forest. But on the other side, a field of yellow oats bent in the breeze.

Several deer slipped out of the oat field and vanished in the woods.

"They come every night," the Owl told Gurri.

A song of joy rose into the sky.

"It's the Lark," the Owl spoke again.

It was day, and the Owl was sleepy. Hiding his eyes beneath his wing, he was asleep.

Soon Gurri was no longer afraid of HIM, for HE brought her clover. She found the Owl was a lure. The crows came to call insults, and tease the Owl. And all the Owl could do was clack his beak at them. But the man shot them.

BAMBI had not been seen. Faline was worried. Never had she gone so long without news of him. Had something happened to him?

"No," Perri told her. "We squirrels have heard no news of any killing."

The Screech-Owl said wisely, "Bambi is looking for Gurri. But that rain washed Man's footprints away."

Bambi did nothing rash. He was the Prince: he had to think of the herd. Always he set foot with care. Always he used all his woodcraft to see and hear, but not be seen.

When he reached the edge of the forest, he stopped. To venture into that open country, with no place to hide, would be like plunging into deep water when you cannot swim.

For three days he watched and waited for Gurri. Then he made up his mind. He must show himself. Then, while the man pursued him, perhaps Gurri could escape. Only a hero would have risked so much.

One evening he found a path where the man scent clung.
Nose to the ground, Bambi followed where it led. The dog
Hector barked, and Bambi froze. With ears pricked forward
to catch the slightest sound, he stood sorting out the odors on
the breeze. That was the Dog, and that, perhaps, the Owl. He
came a few steps closer—Gurri! With one bound Bambi cleared
the fence and stood beside her.

"Father!" she sobbed, when she looked up and saw him.

"My child!" he whispered.

The Owl watched in silence.

Bambi eyed the fence. "Can you jump that high?"

"Never," the Owl declared. "Whoo-hoo!"

Bambi spun about, but Gurri told him, "He's a prisoner, too."

"Try, now, to jump over the fence," Bambi urged her.

Gurri ran and jumped, but the fence was too high. She tried again.

"That's the spirit!" Bambi told her. "Watch, now!"

He cleared the fence with ease.

Gurri tried and tried, but her legs were too short. She couldn't make it. And it was almost daylight.

"I'll come back tonight," Bambi promised. "Don't lose heart, my little one."

His hoofs drummed on the hard ground as he sped for the shelter of the trees.

When the man came with a load of clover for Gurri, he saw the new hoof prints. "A buck!" he said. "And what a fellow! I'd like a shot at him!"

"All right, your wound is healed." He opened the gate. But Gurri couldn't move.

When HE was gone, though, she whispered goodbye to the Owl. Then she raced across the field. Soon the forest hid her in its shadows.

Bambi was waiting. They trotted home together.

Bright eyes peered at them from every branch. The Woodpecker made a sound like the roll of little drums. Word went through the forest, "Bambi has brought her back."

Gurri was tired. But when she had greeted her mother and Geno, and napped awhile, she was her own gay self.

Indian summer came. Berries ripened, leaves turned red, and acorns fell. Perri, the squirrel, worked all day harvesting her winter's food supply. Geno and Gurri liked acorns, too.

"The time of ease is nearly over," Faline told them. "Winter will soon be here. When the leaves fall, men come with thunder-sticks, and it is well to know where to hide."

ONE MORNING Boso's mother came racing toward them. She was panting hard. "Is Boso here?" she gasped.

"Why, no," Faline told her.

"He's gone!" Rolla gasped.

"We'll all search for him," Geno told her.

"Let's each go a different way." Gurri slipped quietly away.

The forest was very still. Songbirds had left for the South.

Then Gurri found him. Boso lay, his head caught in a snare. He couldn't speak. The noose was too tight around his neck.

Gurri's cries brought the others, but they couldn't free the trapped fawn.

Then came a sound of heavy footsteps. "It is *HE!*" They fled in terror. But Gurri watched from behind a bush, for she knew that voice.

"Why, for the love of Pete . . . !" The Gamekeeper went down on one knee. "Those poachers again!" he growled.

32

With gentle fingers he freed Boso. The young deer gasped for air. "That's it, take it easy," the man told him.

Boso staggered to his feet, then stumbled away.

Now the man hid behind a tree. By and by another man came, and knelt to examine the snare.

The Gamekeeper stepped into view. "All right, the jig's up! We don't want poaching around here. I'm taking you in."

"You—and who else?" snarled the Poacher. His gun went off.

The Gamekeeper sprang. His great fist shot out, and the poacher fell to the ground.

Gurri ran for safety.

"Now get going!" said the Gamekeeper. He and the poacher went together, leaving the forest in peace.

The news ran through the tree-tops: "Two He's were fighting. It was for Boso. Boso is safe."

THE ELKS fought through the forest, their antlers clicking.

"This is the time," said Bambi, "for us to keep out of their way. Don't cross their path."

He faded into the shadows—not an instant too soon. For a great stag had entered the clearing. Behind him came his five wives.

Faline's hair pricked as the great elk threw his head back and roared his challenge. "We'd better go now," she whispered.

Geno glanced across the clearing. "No," he told her. "We're safer not to move."

From across the clearing another stag came, a great elk with a crown of sixteen points. He seemed younger than the first one. The five wives looked first at one, then at the other. They would follow whichever won the fight.

Darkness had come. The harvest moon rose behind the trees. The ground lay bathed in silver between the naked tree trunks.

35

Suddenly the two stags rushed at each other. There was a
clash as their antlers struck together. Breathing hard, they
circled each other. They clashed again.

Faline whispered, "We must go," and stole away. Geno followed, but Gurri stayed to watch.

Now they struggled with heaving chests, their horns inter-
laced. Suddenly the old one swung his head and gave the
other a fearful blow in the side. The young stag turned and
ran for his life. The winner raised his head and roared his
triumph.

Gurri turned for home, but the young stag had seen her. Angry, he wanted to hurt someone. He charged.

Gurri ran, squeezing between the tree trunks where he could not follow. The crack of a shot stopped the elk.

Bambi met her sternly. "You almost paid the price," he said.

The time came when the air was like an icy pool. The leaves fell from the trees and piled in drifts. Crisp and dry, they crackled under even the lightest foot. "When it rains," Faline told the deer, "leaves turn soft, and our feet make no sound."

Soon the rain came, a steady downpour. Life now was cold discomfort for the deer. Their winter coats matched the brown leaves. The grass had lost its sweet taste, but the deer had to eat it or starve.

Geno seemed to hear the trees talking. "Well," said the Oak, "another summer over! I'll be taking a long nap." The Beech yawned. "I'll be joining you."

The pool was icy around the edges, and Geno had to breathe hard on the ice to get a drink.

Faline sampled the still air. "Snow!" she said.

A pale flake lighted on Geno's nose. Softly the flakes came floating through the darkness. In three days the snow lay belly-deep. Now the deer had to scrape and scrape to find even a mouthful of anything to eat. They all grew thin.

Finally HE came. He built long shelters, with racks under them, and filled the racks with dried clover. The elks came first. Faline and the children waited till they had eaten. Then they feasted. Surely HE was good to them! But Faline couldn't forget the thunder-stick. "Best to hide when HE comes," she told her children.

There were long weeks of cold. Then sunshine warmed the air, and the snow gleamed till Geno and Gurri were half blinded. Soon melting snow made little rivers of the forest paths.

38

One morning Bambi came. "Hunters are here," he warned them. "Follow me." Unlike most bucks at this time of year, he still had his antlers.

Faline, trembling, fell in behind him. Geno pretended he was not afraid. Gurri was excited.

After a time Bambi told them: "Now we must separate. Hide, and when the hunters come, just act like rocks. Don't move. Don't even breathe."

The day wore on. At last came the sound of voices. "Remember, gentlemen," the Gamekeeper said, "no large game today! And leave the owls alone."

The hunters came. A horn sounded. Another answered. The pheasants broke from cover. Bang! Bang! Guns spoke.

"Keep your heads down," Faline whispered.

Geno was too cold to move. "All right," said Bambi at last. "Get up now." Geno's legs were numb with cold. The men had gone. Dusk spun its first thin webs, and with it came still peace.

A pheasant with a broken wing tried to fly to safety. "HE will find her," Bambi whispered.

Then they saw him stop. Stretched on the ground lay a deer. "Are you badly hurt?" Bambi asked. Then they saw. — It was too late to help. They moved on, their hearts sad.

Now they heard a voice calling for help. It was Boso's mother. She had been shot. "It's my leg," she told them. "It's not too bad. But I wish you'd look for the children and make sure they're safe."

"We'll find Boso and Lana for you," Faline assured her. They hurried on. They found the two fawns feeding at the clover rack. The two dashed away to find their mother.

Faline and her own children were hungry. They must eat to live. But Bambi left them. He had other work to do.

Snow fell on snow again. The wind shrieked, and deep snow banked in the forest. The trees wore icicles. But the Gamekeeper came with armloads of food for the forest folk.

It was the closed season, a time of peace for them. The deer searched now in daylight, but found little grass.

Bambi had lost his crown. His great antlers had fallen, but they would grow again.

42

IT WAS EVENING. Purple shadows crept across the snow. The Screech-Owl sat on a sleeping oak, his feathers blown up about him for warmth. "You'd better look out," he warned. "The Wolf-Dog is about."

"The dog? Hector?" Gurri asked.

"No, Nero. He's twice as big." The Owl clacked his beak. "What's more, he's part wolf."

"Wolf?" Faline gasped in terror. "I didn't know there were ever wolves in this forest."

"There aren't. But Nero is," snapped the Owl. "He belongs in the village, but his master is sick-a-bed, and Nero goes hunting on his own." He told how the huge beast had a ruff of fur around his neck, and howled sometimes like a wolf.

Two days later Nero killed his first deer. The victim was a doe. It was dusk, and he stalked her in silence, as a wolf does. Just like the wolf his great-grandfather had been.

Every creature in the forest trembled at his howl.

Again the forest rang with the wolf call, and again Nero had killed a doe.

The third time Nero gave the wolf call, Rolla was moving lamely about, Lana and Boso not far from their mother. Nero began circling to get behind her. — In the nick of time, she leaped out of his way. True to their teaching, the fawns ran, one to the right and one to the left.

Had Rolla's leg been healed, she might have outrun the Wolf-Dog even then. But it was hard for her to jump the drifts. She must fall back on a trick she knew.

Turning quickly, she butted Nero in the shoulder. As he fell, she dashed away.

To her surprise, she ran straight into Bambi's little family. Nero followed.

Faline and Gurri were too frightened to move. But Geno ran. Nero ran after the one that moved.

Blindly through the woods ran Geno. He cleared the snowbanks with great leaps. Now his speed came into play. His belly whitened with the snow it scraped. His breath blew behind him, freezing to tiny points of smoke.

Geno was young. But he was weak with winter's hunger. His legs tired, and his lungs gave out.

"Help!" he cried at last. "Help!"

BAMBI had come down from his cave on the hillside. As usual, he was headed up-wind. He tested the air from habit. Here the Hare had passed, and there the Squirrel had a winter hoard. Bambi sorted out each smell.

He stopped suddenly. This was a fresh scent on the breeze. It was the strong odor of a killer!

Bambi pricked his ears forward to the message the wind brought him. He held his breath to listen.

In that moment he heard Geno's call for help.

Bambi's great muscles flexed. He sprang, his ears flattened to the wind. The trees flew past him.

Just one big leap lay between the Wolf-Dog and Geno. Bambi cut between them. Amazed, the Wolf-Dog stopped, his forelegs braced.

Bambi fell. He got up limping. That is the way the pheasant mother protects her chicks: While the foe makes after her, they have a chance to hide.

While Geno raced on to safety, his father stumbled. The Wolf-Dog sprang for him.

Just beyond his jaws, Bambi led him on. Faster now, the chase was on, but muscles matched. And Bambi's wild-craft was better than the Dog's, for the Dog had spent his life, till now, by the hearth.

On through the forest, up the hill, around a turn — and
one great leap carried Bambi to his hidden cave.

The Wolf-Dog sprang, but could not reach the cave mouth.
It was too high. Again he tried the jump, and again. Then he
waited.

Bambi waited, too. The moon rose, and the giant elk came
to nibble their supper.

48

A young Stag that looked like Bambi came nibbling the tender bark of the young trees. The Wolf-Dog crept behind him. The Stag, leaping for safety, backed against the hillside.

The Wolf-Dog sprang. The Stag reared on his hind legs and struck sharp blows with his hoofs. The Wolf-Dog sprang again.

The Stag, rearing almost upright, slipped on the ice. Nero's jaws snapped. That was the end for the Stag.

Next day the Gamekeeper came, his high boots crunching in the snow. Bambi was still in his cave, and he lay still, though he sniffed and listened.

The man stopped. He had found Nero's paw marks, and his victim. "A *wolf?*" he asked himself. "No, it's that dog from the village. He has become a *killer*."

He followed Nero's trail through the snow. Day after day he watched. Then he saw a gray form skulking through the bushes. It was the Wolf-Dog. He was chasing the Hare.

The Gamekeeper raised his gun and fired. He aimed for the dog's rump — and his aim was good. Nero yelped, and ran. It would be a long time before Nero could sit down with comfort. His tail went between his legs, and his ears drooped.

"Go home!" the Gamekeeper told him, "or you'll get it again."

The forest saw Nero no more.

GENO was lost. When the sun rose, he traveled with his shadow straight ahead of him. That way, he should come out *somewhere*, not just circle. At last a Jay lighted on a twig above him. "Geno!" the bird shrieked.

Then Faline called, "Geno! You're safe!"

Gurri danced over to him. "How did you escape the Wolf-Dog?"

Geno told what had happened. "Father came like the wind. Then the Wolf-Dog chased *him*."

"Bambi is safe," Faline assured them. "The birds have seen him."

Lana, the other girl fawn, called, "Geno! We're so glad you're back!"

Geno dug at the snow with his forehoof.

"Quite the hero, aren't you?" Lana's brother Boso mocked.

Geno turned to go.

"Let's not quarrel," Lana called.

Yet there was a coldness between Boso and Geno after that.

In time the snow melted, and the sun shone warm again. Hillsides were blue with violets. Brooks tinkled, and the ground was soft. The air was filled with the song of birds building their nests.

The deer were trotting to the meadow at sunset when Gurri called, "Mother, look at Geno's head."

"What's the matter with it?" Geno asked.

"It's got two bumps on it," Gurri told him.

Faline smiled. "Yes, he's growing up. Those are the beginnings of his antlers."

"Antlers!" Geno was amazed.

"Yes. Some day you will look just like your father," Faline told him.

Geno strutted along the path, his head held high.

Gurri called, "Lana, look! Geno's getting his crown."

"He always did have a swelled head," Boso said sourly.

One day Geno found two young bucks in the meadow. They told him their mother had been killed and their father, too. They were orphans. Their names were Nello and Membo.

"I am Geno, the son of Bambi," he told them, proudly.

Faline had a kind heart. "Wouldn't you like to stay with us?" she asked them.

The orphans were only too glad to be adopted.

From then on, Geno was their leader.

Now the Oak wore lacy green. The meadow was sweet with young grass. The Woodpecker drummed, birds sang, and

bees visited the clover. The deer lost their winter coats and wore red again. And Geno grew two horns, each the size of a finger. They were covered with a mossy skin.

How the young fellows raced and played, bucking, stopping on stiffened legs!

When at last Bambi came to see them, his own new antlers were full grown. The horn gleamed like ivory. He nuzzled Faline fondly.

The orphans stood straight and still. Bambi looked them over. "So," he said at last, "we have two adopted sons. Welcome!"

Nello and Membo were happy.

"Now," Bambi told them, "I want both of you and Geno to come with me." He led them to a low branch. "Strip that moss off your antlers," he bade them. He showed them how to rub their antlers clean.

At last their tiny horns shone clear. "But don't fight," he warned them. Then he said goodbye.

Geno was restless now. One day he met Lana. "Your horns are very handsome," she told him softly.

Geno felt his chest expand.

Unheard, Boso stepped up behind him. "Want a fight?"

"What for?" asked Geno.

"Because I don't like your looks." Boso lowered his head and pawed the ground.

Geno thought, Father told us not to fight.

Boso roared and charged.

Geno spun on his hind hoofs and ran.

"Coward!" yelled Boso.

The next time they met, Geno said, "Boso, I don't want to fight you."

"Huh!" Boso sneered. "The son of Bambi is afraid."

Perri, the squirrel, came swinging through the treetops. "Listen, Geno, a fellow like Boso must have his fight. You've got to make war, to have peace."

Geno saw his sister Gurri talking with a young buck. "You are very lovely," he was telling her.

Just then Lana danced up to him. "You are lovely, too," Geno told her. He didn't see Bambi watching from beyond the bushes.

Boso dashed into the clearing. "Leave my sister alone!" he yelled. He charged.

54

Geno waited till Boso was almost upon him, then stepped
lightly to one side.

Boso charged again. This time Geno waited. Boso fairly
bounced off him.

Head on, they struggled. Boso broke free, but this time
Geno ran to meet him. Their heads cracked together. Boso
almost fell. Geno charged again. This time Boso landed on
his back.

Geno stood breathing hard. Then he said, "Well, Boso, we've
had our fight. Now let's be friends."

But Boso refused to answer.

Bambi rubbed his antlers thoughtfully against a tree. He
was glad Geno had won the fight. But he was even more glad
his son had tried *not* to fight.

ONE DAY Geno was drinking at the pool. It was shadowed by tall ferns. Two ducks were teaching their little ones to swim. "Wa-ak, wa-ak!" one mother called, and three small yellow ducklings made a left-hand turn.

"Wa-ak, wa-a-a-a-ak," the other told her ducklings, and they swam in single file. The mothers wagged their tails.

Suddenly a shot rang out. Perri hastened down a tree. "Why, I've been shot at!"

Bambi had overheard. "You smaller animals and birds must all be careful," he told them. "The killer is a Boy. He doesn't aim well, but he does keep trying."

"This is not the hunting season," the Gamekeeper had said. But the Boy didn't care.

The golden days of summer passed. "The time has come," Bambi told his family, "to sleep by day, and take the forest paths when darkness falls." He turned to Geno. "Will you do that, my son?"

Geno understood that now it must be he who led Faline and the fawns when evening came.

56

At last, one morning, shots rang out again. The Boy! Who was he after now?

Since Boso had lost the fight, he had walked alone. So it was that he came home from the salt-lick after the sun was up.

The Boy with the rifle saw him. He tiptoed from bush to bush. A twig snapped beneath his shoe. Boso started. He felt danger was near.

The boy fired. Boso leaped, but the bullet burned his chest.

Bambi, on guard as usual, sprang to his feet. He met Boso in a grove of pine trees. "Come!" Bambi told him. Boso wanted to lie down, but he obeyed. The blood dripping from his chest made sticky tracks on the pine needles.

"Hurry," Bambi urged. "We must stop that bleeding."

They came to a spring where a strange herb grew. The gray-green weed smelled like bitter stuff. "Eat that," Bambi commanded.

Boso took a mouthful, but spat it out.

"Eat!" Bambi ordered. "It will stop the bleeding. Then the Boy can't track you."

After losing Boso, the Boy came every day to hunt. He wanted to shoot a buck.

But now the Gamekeeper came on the run. "What are you up to?" he demanded. "Didn't I tell you to leave the fawns alone?"

The Boy sneered. "I always do as I please."

The Gamekeeper smacked him sharply.

Perri brought the news. "Boso is wounded, but Bambi is helping him."

"Was Boso hurt?" Gurri sprang to her feet. But sudden rain began to fall. How could she find him?

One night, when the stars were out, Boso came to see them. He had a long scar across his chest. "Listen, Geno," he said, "why don't we all go to the meadow and play?"

"Let's!" they all agreed.

"Gurri," Faline whispered, "where do you suppose your father is? It's been so long . . ."

Ever since the shooting, Bambi had watched, and trailed the Boy everywhere he went. Sometimes he would send Perri the squirrel with a word of warning when the Boy prowled too near. For now the Boy had stolen his father's big gun, and his aim was better.

This night the Boy was later than usual. He happened on the meadow where the young deer played.

The Boy watched from behind a tree. His gun was ready.

But Bambi watched behind the Boy. How could he warn those youngsters in the meadow?

To dash past the Boy would be certain death. And the Boy's gun could speak more than once. It would be death for Bambi and for some of the herd.

The Boy had his eyes on Geno, the buck with the largest antlers. Yes, Geno would do, he told himself.

Silently the Boy killer steadied himself on one knee. He lifted the gun.

At that moment Bambi acted. Lowering his antlers, he charged the Boy. His antlers drove straight at the Boy's back.

The Boy yelled. The gun spoke, but the bullet went wild. It flew up into the treetop.

Bambi leaped straight over the Boy, and was gone—in the shadows of the forest.

At the sound, Geno and the other young deer on the meadow fled to safety.

"Bambi attacked the Boy!" the Screech Owl cried as he flew. "Bambi attacked the Boy!"

The forest woke. The news spread in a chorus of chirps and squeaks. "Bambi attacked the Boy!"

The Boy ran home and took to his bed. He had had enough of hunting for a long, long time.

FALINE was alone in the clearing. Suddenly Bambi was at her side.

"The time has come," he told her.

Faline's voice quivered. "But it's hard to see them go."

"I know. But don't you remember how it was with us? Don't worry. You will find the right words to tell them."

"And you," Faline said, "—will you be leaving me too?"

Bambi nuzzled her fondly. "You know better than that, Faline. The children must be taught the ways of the forest, the secrets of woodcraft. But very soon I shall come back for you."

And what he said made Faline happy as she watched him go.

Down beside the pool, Boso was telling Gurri, "I'll never be handsome, with this scar."

"You are very modest," Gurri told him, her eyes shining in the moonlight.

Lana was whispering to Geno, "You are very brave."

The Owl's cry came, "Hah-ah, hah-aha!"

"Let's find Mother," Geno said.

Faline looked them all over proudly. "What a lovely family!"

"We'll never leave you," Gurri said.

Faline smiled. "Oh, yes, you will. You are grown up, you know. Why, just look at Geno's crown!"

Geno said, "Are you sending us away?"

"That's right," Faline told them gently.

"No!" exclaimed Membo.

"Yes, my son. You and Nello are grown up, too. You don't need me any longer. You, Gurri, will go, and Geno too."

Geno looked up quickly. He saw a shadow moving in the morning mist.

"Father," he cried, "will you teach me the ways of the forest, how to move in it like a shadow as you do . . .?"

"Yes," said Bambi. "Find your sleeping place now, and when night falls we'll begin."

When it was dark Faline, standing alone, could hear them as they passed her: Geno's hooves, the lighter steps of Gurri, and the brothers slowly stepping in time like a single animal.

Faline felt happy. All the children of the forest came to the time of leaving, but hers were good children and they would come again.

"They go," she murmured to the finches, "and the better they are, the more we miss them. But they must go. That is something that all parents know."

She looked up. A well-beloved shadow moved where the mist was thickest. It was Bambi. With a light heart she went toward him.